Fearless Fiona

The Mothproof Hall Mystery
and The Purple Poodle Mystery

Also by Karen Wallace in Happy Cat Books

The Mystery of the Great Stone Haggis
Snapper Bites Back

Fearless Fiona

The Mothproof Hall Mystery
and The Purple Poodle Mystery

Karen Wallace

Illustrated by Judy Brown

HAPPY CAT BOOKS

To another Fearless Fiona, with thanks

Published by
Happy Cat Books
An imprint of Catnip Publishing Ltd
14 Greville Street
London
EC1N 8SB

This edition first published 2007
3 5 7 9 10 8 6 4 2

A CIP catalogue record for this book is available from
the British Library

ISBN 978-1-905117-45-1

Printed in Poland

www.catnippublishing.co.uk

Contents

The Mothproof Hall Mystery

Chapter One

"Whaddyamean my paper's run out of money?"

shouted Mr Metalpress, editor of the *Daily Screamer*, to Mr Stinge the Bank Manager. "All we need is a good story."

Mr Metalpress banged down the telephone. Then he banged his head on his desk.

His secretary opened the door. "Did you bang, sir?" she asked sweetly.

"I certainly did," said Mr Metalpress. "Get me Fearless Fiona, fast!"

Fearless Fiona was a part-time reporter on the *Daily Screamer*. She was also the only daughter of Mr Metalpress. When she was a baby her father had wrapped her in copies of the *Daily Screamer* instead of frilly pink blankets. That is, when Mrs Metalpress wasn't looking. Now, nine years later, Fearless had a bloodhound's nose for news and her stories were always the best.

For her last birthday, Mr Metalpress had given her a mobile phone

specially adapted to fit on her
mountain bike.

"I might need to get you in a hurry,"
he had said.

Now, that phone was ringing. "Yes,
chief," said Fearless, steering her
bike expertly behind a hedge so
no-one could listen in on their
conversation.

"Fearless, I need your help," said Mr
Metalpress. "The paper's in trouble.
The bank want to close it down."

"We need one good story, and you're
the person to get it."

"Shoot," said Fearless, grimly.

"Last Saturday, a priceless collection
of rubies was stolen from Mothproof
Hall," said Mr Metalpress. "Find out
who did it, Fearless. It could be our
breakthrough."

"I'll talk to Lord Mothproof right away, chief, er, Dad," said Fearless, turning her bike as she spoke. "You can count on me."

As she sped back down the hill, her eyes were dark and thoughtful behind the big glasses with the bright blue frames. This was going to be the big one, she knew it.

Mothproof Hall looked like a cutout castle on the back of a cereal packet. Fearless Fiona raced up the drive and did an expert skid stop on the gravel in front of a greenhouse that sat like a huge glass birthday cake beside the

main house.

Immediately the front door of the house swung open and a greasy-looking man wearing a gold earring and black tail-coat came down the steps. He was carrying a large bag labelled *Meaty Snacks*.

"Can I help you, little lady?" he said

in a whining voice. "Sidney Grabbit, butler, at your service."

"I would like to speak to Lord Mothproof, please," said Fearless. She did not like the look of this strange man nor did she like being called 'little lady'.

"Lord Mothproof's a very busy man, little lady," said the butler. "I'm sure I could assist."

"Thank you," said Fearless. "But I must speak to his lordship personally. It's about the missing rubies."

"Is it now?" said Sidney Grabbit, pulling his earring and looking at Fearless more closely.

"Gwabbit!" A voice creaked like a rusty hinge from inside the greenhouse. Lord Mothproof appeared at the door.

He was tall and stooping and wore
an old raincoat that came down to his
ankles. "Have you got them?"

"Yes, your worshipful," said Grabbit,
handing him the bag labelled *Meaty
Snacks*.

Fearless Fiona stepped forward and introduced herself. "May I ask you a few questions, sir?" she said, taking a small notebook from her satchel.

"Of course you may," said Lord Mothproof. "I like questions. Come into the gweenhouse." He turned to the butler who was pretending to polish the plastic doorknob with

his coat tail. "Thank you, Gwabbit, that will be all," he said, and firmly closed the door.

Fearless caught the look in Sidney Grabbit's eyes. Definitely shifty, she said to herself.

Inside the greenhouse, the air was hot and wet. Classical music was playing. All around there

were hundreds of strange red–tongued plants.

Even stranger were the sticky spines that grew along the edge of the red tongues. She watched as Lord Mothproof reached into the bag of Meaty Snacks and placed a small brown lump on the first tongue. At first nothing happened. Lord Mothproof made a cooing sound and gently tickled the plant's thick hairy stem. "Tea time, chewub," he said softly.

At the sound of his voice, the spiny sides of the red tongue curled round the brown lump. Then there was a loud burp.

Lord Mothproof chuckled. "My pwide and joy," he said, tickling its thick green stem. "They'll eat anything, you know."

"Now, what are these questions?"

"It's about Lady Mothproof's rubies," said Fearless. "When did you first notice they were missing?" As she spoke some of the plants made

crumping noises. Others rubbed their long stems against Lord Mothproof's raincoat like hungry cats.

"Why, after the Mozart," said Lord Mothproof.

"What Mozart?" asked Fearless.

"The Mozart concert on Saturday, of course." said Lord Mothproof. He began to hum a tune that Fearless didn't recognize.

"Mozart?" said Fearless, trying to keep the conversation going. So far she hadn't discovered any clues at all. Lord Mothproof shook his head.

"It's the *Meaty Snacks* jingle," he said. "Rather good, don't you think?"

Fearless nodded. She had never heard of it. "About Lady Mothproof's rubies," she said firmly.

"Ah, yes the rubies," said Lord

Mothproof. "They live in bowls by the piano."

"Remind her of fruit gums, she says. Red ones were her favourite," he stopped. "I'm not speaking too quickly, I hope," he said. He peered down at the funny shapes she was writing in the notebook. "What's that?"

"I write shorthand," said Fearless.

"Do you now?" said Lord Mothproof, staring at her fingers. He opened his mouth to say something.

"You said 'Red ones were her favourite'," said Fearless desperately.

"Quite right!" said Lord Mothproof. "Of course, she's not allowed them any more. Doctor's orders. Well, after the Mozart, the bowls were empty. That is to say, the rubies were gone."

A voice like a hunting horn rattled the windows. "Marmaduke!"

"Yes, dear," said his Lordship to no one in particular.

"Marmaduke!" Fearless looked around her but could see no one. Then a curtain of hanging vines was pushed aside and a big blonde woman strode up the aisle. She was wearing a flowing cotton beach dress printed with palm trees, and on her head was something that looked very like a pineapple. In front of her she pushed an old-fashioned buggy with an enormous watermelon propped up on a pillow inside.

"My wife," said Lord Mothproof to Fearless.

"Isn't he boootiful?" cried Lady Mothproof.

"Who?" said Fearless, looking from one to the other.

"The watermelon, don't you know," said Lord Mothproof.

Lady Mothproof parked the watermelon to one side and patted it lovingly. "Just LOVES his liquid feed!" she cooed.

"About the rubies," said Fearless.

"Quite!" boomed Lady Mothproof. "About the rubies! Marmaduke, I have taken steps! I am offering a reward!"

A reward, thought Fearless. That would would help the newspaper! She picked up her notebook and put on her double-strength-to-dislodge-the-stubbornest-stories reporter's voice. "Have you any idea how they were stolen, Lady Mothproof?" she said.

Lady Mothproof responded immediately. "How? No! When? Yes!" she said, firmly. "I say, aren't you Fiona Jane Metalpress?"

Fearless nodded.

"Daughter of the editor of the *Daily Screamer* and star reporter?"

Fearless nodded.

"Jolly good show," boomed Lady Mothproof. "I suppose you'd like to look around the house, ask a few questions, that sort of thing?"

"May I?" said Fearless.

"Of course you may, my dear," said Lady Mothproof. "And while you're there, go and see Crinoline and Lacy in the nursery. They would absolutely love it!"

Fearless Fiona's heart sank. Crinoline and Lacy were the Mothproofs' daughters.

They were well known to be the biggest sissies that ever lived. Last time she had been sent to visit them,

she had locked herself in their wendy house to get out of playing dolly hairdressers. The time before that they had forced her to dress up in a pinafore and frilly cap to play dinner at the palace.

They had been princesses. She had been the maid. "We'll change places next time," Crinoline had said. But Fearless hadn't stayed that long. Still, it was all in the line of duty, she told herself. Anyway, they just might have some clues.

"And you are coming to the Mozart, of course," said Lady Mothproof.

"Of course," said Fearless, quickly. This could be the breakthrough she needed.

"You can keep an eye on my emeralds," added Lady Mothproof.

"Emeralds?" said Fearless.

"Not as comforting as rubies," said Lady Mothproof. "They remind me of red fruit gums, you know. But green ones are my second favourite, so the emeralds will have to do. One must be thankful for small mercies. Don't you agree, Marmaduke?"

"Yes, dear," said her husband.

Just then Fearless noticed that Sydney Grabbit was listening at the door. Lord Mothproof followed her eyes and saw him, too

"Stwange man, Gwabbit," he said.
"Absolutely no manners, at all. Fwom
Bognor, don't you know?"

They watched as Grabbit began
polishing the plastic doorknob with his
tail-coat.

"Do butlers often come from
Bognor?" asked Fearless.

"No," said Lord Mothproof,
absentmindedly popping a Meaty
Snack into his mouth.

Chapter Two

The nursery was at the top of the house. Fearless climbed the stairs with a heavy heart.

"Why *not* birds eating cherries?" shouted an angry voice from the other side of a door. "He's supposed to be Governor of the Bank of England."

"Because *she's* hired the best interior decorator from Knightsbridge and birds eating cherries are old hat! Don't you know anything?" There was a sound of ripping wallpaper.

"Well, I get to choose the bathroom," said the first voice, sounding sulky. "And they're having GOLD TAPS!"

Fearless opened the door. Crinoline and Lacy were sitting in front of an enormous dolls' house. Crinoline, the eldest, held a swatch of materials in her hand. Her younger sister clutched a grey-suited doll which

she was squashing into a miniature Rolls Royce.

That must be the Governor of the Bank of England, thought Fearless. She felt sorry for him.

"Hi, Crinoline. Hi, Lacy," she said, sitting on the edge of the armchair nearest the door.

"Gosh!" cried Crinoline. "Fearless! What are you doing here? We were just about to choose the curtains."

"Do you want to play?" asked Lacy. "You could be Clarissa."

"Who's Clarissa?"

"It's Friday," said Lacy. "Clarissa's come to cook the D.P. *If* the curtains are ready." She shot a malevolent look at her sister.

"D.P.?" said Fearless.

"Dinner party, of course," said Lacy.

"Don't you know anything?"

Fearless had to remind herself she
was on a job.

"Sorry," she said, as nicely as she
could. "I don't have time to play right

now. I'm trying to find out who took the rubies."

"Oh, them," said the two sisters.

"You might be able to do me a favour," said Fearless.

"We like favours," said Crinoline.

She opened her hand. In it was a doll dressed in a white pinafore with a frilly cap. "Friday's not the same without Clarissa," she said meaningfully.

"What do you want to know?" said Lacy as Crinoline set up a miniature dining-room table.

Fearless took a deep breath and pulled out her notebook.

"Who was at the Mozart last week?" she said.

Crinoline smiled prettily and put the doll on the floor near Fearless.

"The Pineapple Appreciation Society," said Lacy. "Friends of Mummy's, you know."

"Of course," said Fearless, scribbling in her notebook. "Who's invited tomorrow?"

"Local big-wigs, Daddy says," said Crinoline.

Just the people the *Daily Screamer* needs to impress, thought Fearless. "Does anyone else enter the concert room?" she asked.

"Grub brings in the plants," said Lacy.

"What?" said Fearless.

"Daddy's plants, of course. He always invites some of his plants," said Crinoline.

Fearless's mouth hung open.

"To listen to Mozart?" she said.

"He says they like it," said Lacy. "What's so strange about that?" she added, staring hard at Fearless.

"Nothing at all," said Fearless quickly. This was becoming the most difficult story she had ever investigated, but she knew it was the most important one. She *had* to crack it.

"So who's Grub anyway?" she said, casually.

"He's the gardener," said Lacy.

"Has he worked for Lord Mothproof a long time?" asked Fearless.

"No," said Crinoline. "He came at the same time as Grabbit." She looked at her watch. "I say," she said abruptly. "Too late for Clarissa's D.P. It's teatime. Lacy! Ring the bell!"

"Do stay, Fearless," cried Lacy.

"We always have soft boiled eggs and warm milk."

"And we watch *The Sound of Music*," added Crinoline. "This will be the 402nd time we've seen it!"

They rushed over to a little table that sat in front of the television.

Fearless stared at the tiny doll with the white cap which lay at the her feet. It was all she could do not to grind its silly face into the carpet. She edged towards the door.

"Sorry, I have to go now," she muttered quickly. "Thanks for your help."

But Crinoline and Lacy weren't listening. They were busy tying napkins round their necks and arguing over who would have the rabbit egg-cup.

Outside the nursery door, Fearless took a deep breath of fresh air. For the first time in her life, she was grateful to the people who made *The Sound of Music*. She looked down at the notes she had taken.

Crinoline and Lacy hadn't been particularly helpful . . .

Fearless thought for a moment. Could it be possible . . . Then she thought of the soft boiled eggs, the warm milk . . . No, she decided. It couldn't be possible.

The mystery of the missing rubies was still not solved. Outside, her bicycle was still leaning against the greenhouse.

Inside, a man was filling a watering can. That must be Mr Grub, she thought.

She crept up to the door to get a closer look at him.

A low growling noise seemed to be coming from the plants. It got louder as the gardener went towards them. Suddenly, one of them leaned over and bit him. With a shout he dropped the can and shook his fist at the rows of waving red tongues.

Fearless pedalled down the drive as fast as she could. Those plants hate that man, she thought. I wonder why.

An
hour before
the recital, Mothproof
Hall stood black and silent
under a big moon. Nobody
saw a slim figure in a white
leather cat-suit pedal softly
up the drive.

Fearless wheeled her bike across the grass to the side greenhouse. Suddenly she froze! Grub was standing a few feet in front of her. He turned. At that moment a thick lump of cloud covered the moon. He didn't see her.

Fearless's heart banged so loud in her chest she felt sure he would hear it. She ducked behind a hedge just before the moon slid into the sky once more. Now she could see Grub was carrying a basket. In it there was set of screwdrivers and spanners, a remote control device with an aerial and a large pack of batteries. Not exactly gardening equipment, thought Fearless.

Her newshound's nose began to twitch. She knew she must follow him. It was her last chance to solve the mystery.

Grub set off towards the potting shed. Fearless followed him, taking the short cut round behind the bushes. There was a light on at the window. She peered inside.

Grabbit was there with his back to her, bent over a table. Then she heard Grub stump up the steps and yank open the door. She had to duck so he wouldn't see her.

"Did you bring the batteries?" said Grabbit.

" 'Course I did," said Grub.

"We'll have those emeralds, then we're off," said Grabbit. "This butler stuff's getting right up my nose."

" 'Spose you'd prefer being bitten by them crazy plants of his," sneered Grub.

"Okay, okay," said Grabbit. "Give me a hand with these batteries, will you?" Fearless crouched in the darkness.

What on earth were they talking about? She would

only find out if she could see what they were doing. And time was running out. The concert was due to begin in a few minutes.

Then she remembered her bike pump! Not so much a bike pump as a periscope!

As fast as she could, she crept back around the bushes to get it. Outside the potting shed again, she slowly eased the narrow tube out of its casing, and raised it up to the window's edge.

In the round mirror she saw Grub and Grabbit sitting at the table.

She moved the mirror forwards and saw they were each sitting in front of a tray of Lord Mothproof's plants. At first the plants looked identical. She twisted the mirror

again. Her heart stopped! Grub and Grabbit were fitting batteries into the plant pots!

On the far corner of the table was a square black box with a control lever and three words written below it. She twisted the periscope to get a better look and somehow the viewfinder must have scratched the window pane.

Grub jumped up. "What's that?" he said.

Fearless dropped to the ground. She heard his footsteps stump across the floor towards the window.

"Nothing, you great twitchy twit," said Grabbit. "Now hurry up, we're almost out of time."

The footsteps went back. There

was the scrape of a chair as Grub sat down again.

Fearless eased the periscope back up to the window sill. She knew she was taking a risk but there was no choice. It was now or never. She found the black box again.

The words said

SEARCH AND SWALLOW!

She watched as Grabbit lifted the last plant and fitted it with a battery. "Put them in the same place as last week," he said.

"When you going to switch them on?" said Grub.

"When the lights go out and there's all that coughing and rustling," said Grabbit. "Then we'll pick them up during the interval and make a run for it in the van. Get it?"

"Got it," said Grub.

Below the window, Fearless Fiona's heart thumped with excitement.
So that was how the rubies had disappeared! Grub and Grabbit had substituted robot plants for Lord Mothproof's own ones at the Mozart Concert.

The two plants looked identical except the real ones ate Meaty Snacks while the robots were programmed to swallow rubies and emeralds! No wonder the robbery had seemed so mysterious!

She looked at her watch. Only ten minutes before the recital. She ran back across the lawn and up to the front door. There were lots of

cars outside now. She noticed one in particular, a rusty black van parked at the bottom of the steps.

Lady Mothproof swept into the hall. She was wearing a full-length pineapple-shaped dress with a pineapple handbag. Her long blonde hair was held in place by a jewelled banana. "Sooo glad you're here," cried Lady Mothproof.

"I was beginning to get a teeny weeny bit worried about the . . . you know whats."

"Lady Mothproof," said Fearless breathlessly. "I must . . ."

"Not now, dahling," boomed Lady Mothproof, parking the buggy with one hand and steering Fearless across the floor with the other. "Mozart is almost upon us!"

They went into a room that was half antique shop, half jungle.

Vines with leaves as big as soup plates wrapped themselves round the legs of tables and slithered up the walls and along the ceiling. Carved wooden chairs were

hidden behind green clumps
bursting with purple flowers that
looked as if they were made of
velvet. Palm trees laden with
coconuts and tropical fruit stood
in each corner. And in the middle
of the room, a gleaming white
grand piano seemed to be floating
on four giant lilypads.

Crinoline and Lacy had told her the truth. The room was full of big-wigs. Fearless saw Mr Stinge, the bank manager, sitting in the front row between the Mayor and Mayoress and a plant with long stripy leaves. The headmaster of her school was there. So was the man who owned the printing press where the *Daily Screamer* was made. Other important people peeked out from behind bushes and giant flowers.

Then out of the corner of her eye she saw Grub sidling along the back wall. He was putting the robot plants onto a large table. On the same table were two glass bowls, filled with what looked like green wine gums. The emeralds!

Fearless turned to warn Lady

Mothproof. Then the lights went out. It
was too late.

The audience coughed and rustled
around in their chairs. The pianist sat
down in front of the gleaming white
piano. Fearless watched the robot
plants. This was when Grabbit said he
would switch them on.

At first nothing happened. She hoped against hope that something had gone wrong. But then her stomach turned over.

So slowly, so that they hardly seemed to move at all, the plants began to slither around on the table. Fearless looked to see if anyone else had noticed.

They hadn't. They were all watching the pianist as he flipped his coat tails out behind him and placed his hands above the black and white keyboard.

The first notes rang out across the room.

Silently, the robot plants slid across the table like skaters across ice, searching for the glass bowls. Fearless stared horrified and fascinated as they came to a stop and slowly dipped their spiny red tongues into the mound of emeralds. One by one they swallowed every glittering green lump.

And all the while nobody noticed. After all, who would suspect the plants? It was all fiendishly clever.

But not clever enough, thought Fearless with a grim smile.

When the interval came the audience clapped and cheered. As planned, Grub and Grabbit come smoothly into the room. Fearless watched as they lifted the bulging plants onto a tray. This is it, she thought. There wasn't a moment to lose. She opened her mouth to shout a warning.

"Well if it isn't Miss Fiona Jane Metalpress!" said Mr Stinge, grabbing her hand and pumping it up and down. "So sorry about the paper. Business is business, I'm afraid. Father well?"

"Yes, I mean, no," stammered Fearless. She could feel him staring at her. Rude, just like her father, he would be thinking.

But it was too late for good

manners. Grub and Grabbit were going through the door.

"Excuse me, Mr Stinge," said Fearless, pulling her hand free. She jumped onto a chair.

There was a terrible hush.

"Disgraceful child," muttered Mr Stinge.

"Outrageous behaviour," hissed the Mayoress.

"What's up?" murmured the Mayor, who was a simple man and a little deaf.

All the other important people turned and glared.

"My emeralds!" shrieked Lady Mothproof. "Marmaduke! Do something!"

Fearless ran into the front hall just in time to see Grub racing down the steps towards the rusty van. Grabbit was at the wheel. The engine was running.

I have to stop them! she thought desperately.

If they get away with the jewels, the paper's finished!

Then she saw Lady Mothproof's buggy. It was parked at the top of the steps.

She pointed it at Grub and shoved it forwards.

Bang! Bang! Bang! The buggy bounced down the front steps and tipped out the enormous watermelon. There was a low rumble as the watermelon gathered speed, then a sickening thump as it walloped into the back of Grub's legs.

"Aaargh!" screamed Grub. The tray of robot plants flew into the air.

The watermelon thundered on over the top of Grub and smashed into the front of the van.

Suddenly the sky was full of rubies and emeralds. Hundreds of them spattered down like hailstones onto the gravel.

"My rubies! My emeralds!" shrieked Lady Mothproof. "Dahling! You were wonderful!"

Fearless turned to see her bend down over the watermelon and plant a large kiss on its top end. Not one scratch could be seen on its stripy green skin.

A large man in a blue uniform appeared and helped Grub and Grabbit into the back seat of a police car. Fearless heard the CLICK of handcuffs as the door slammed shut and the car raced away, siren blaring.

For a moment no one spoke.

Mr Stinge, the Mayor and Mayoress and the rest of the important people from the town stood staring down from the front steps.

Lord Mothproof stood staring at the handful of jewels he had picked up from the gravel.

On the top floor, a window opened and Crinoline and Lacy stuck out their heads and stared down at the commotion below. The last notes of *The Sound of Music* could be heard dying away.

"The reward, Marmaduke!" shrieked Lady Mothproof, waving a small yellow envelope. "Give the girl the reward!"

"Yes, dear," said Lord Mothproof. He took the yellow envelope and gave it to Fearless. "And may *I* say, what a simply splendid super sleuth you are!"

Fearless thanked him and took the envelope. Her hands were shaking. As she opened it, she stared straight into the eyes of Mr Stinge. I don't care if he thinks I'm rude, she thought. All I want is to save the *Daily Screamer*.

Then she looked at the small piece of paper she held in her fingers and her face broke into an enormous grin.

It was a cheque for ten thousand pounds!

The Purple Poodle Mystery

Chapter One

shouted Deadline Metalpress, editor
of the *Daily Screamer,* to Beatrice

Daisychain, chairman and managing director of Poodles' Paradise. "What colour is it supposed to be?"

"NOT purple, you nincompoop," snapped Beatrice Daisychain. "Do something, Metalpress, otherwise my chances will be ruined."

Deadline Metalpress had known Beatrice Daisychain for many years. She was the rudest person he had ever met. As far as he was concerned, her chances had been ruined a long time ago. "What chances?" he growled.

"To win the Top Dog Trophy at Krumbs," screeched Beatrice Daisychain. "It's the G-r-reatest Dog Show on earth! It's my life's work! It's my greatest ambition. And it's . . ."

"This evening," interrupted Deadline Metalpress. "Leave it with me."

He banged down the phone and rubbed his boulder-sized head with a heavy hand. For the first time in his life, Deadline Metalpress had

a headache. It was all Beatrice Daisychain's fault. He banged his head on the desk.

His secretary opened the door. "Did you bang, Sir?" she asked sweetly.

"I certainly did," said Deadline Metalpress. "Get me Fearless Fiona, fast!"

Fearless Fiona Metalpress was Deadline's only daughter. When other little girls were taken in their

pushchairs to feed the ducks on the pond, Deadline had taken Fearless to watch copies of the *Daily Screamer* roll off the printing press.

Fearless could still remember the warm inky paper in her hands. Her mother could still remember the black finger marks all over her little white dresses.

Poor Mrs Metalpress! Over the years, she gave up reading her daughter stories about bunnies and princesses.

Instead Fearless kept a stack of old
newspapers by her bed and she knew
most of them by heart.

When she was older, Deadline
Metalpress made his daughter a part-
time reporter on the *Daily Screamer*. She
had a notebook with
her name stamped on
the front. She had a
mountain bike that
could go anywhere.
But most important
of all, her father had
given her a mobile
phone. "When I
need you, I'll need you in a hurry,"
he had growled.

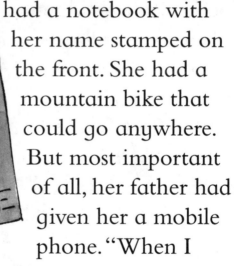

And now that phone was ringing.
Fearless Fiona ducked behind a
hedge and pulled the mobile phone

from its clip on
her mountain
bike.

"Fearless,"
said Deadline
Metalpress in a strangled voice.
"Whaddyaknow about poodles?"

Fearless nearly dropped her
notebook. Her father's voice sounded
very peculiar.

"Poodles?" asked Fearless.

"POODLES!" choked Deadline
Metalpress. "Purple ones!"

Fearless took a deep breath. "Tell me
all about it, Chief, er, Dad," she said
slowly.

"Grrrrr . . ." began Deadline.

"That's right," said Fearless in a
soothing voice. "That's what poodles
say."

There was a sound of banging at the other end of the telephone. It was the only way Deadline could get rid of his headache. A minute later his voice roared down the phone like a concrete mixer on fast forward.

Fearless Fiona heaved a sigh of relief. It was the voice she knew and loved.

"The G-r-reatest Dog Show on

Earth opens this evening," bellowed Deadline Metalpress. "Last night someone poured purple ink over Beatrice Daisychain's prize-winning poodle!"

"That must be Lulu Labelle," gasped Fearless. "She's tipped to win the Top Dog Trophy!"

"Not if she's purple, she won't," yelled Deadline. Then his voice dropped so low the phone juddered. "Get me something for the front page," he muttered. "A good dog story always sells four times as many newspapers. One-extra-for-each-leg."

Fearless grinned. There wasn't anything her dad didn't know about newspapers.

"You can count on me, Chief, er Dad," she said.

Chapter Two

Poodles' Paradise was at the end of a long drive behind wrought iron gates carved to look like two poodles facing each other. Where their noses touched, the gates locked.

Fearless pressed the entry buzzer and explained who she was.

"What took you so long?" snapped a rude voice. The noses popped apart and the gates opened.

Fearless pedalled slowly down the drive. At the far end behind a stone poodle fountain stood a white and pink house with little houses all around it. It looked like an enormous birthday cake surrounded by cup cakes with the same icing.

A woman was standing at the door. She was as wide as she was short and she was wearing something floaty with daisies printed all over it. Long white gloves went up to her elbows. She looked like a pug in a party dress and her name was Beatrice Daisychain.

"So you're Deadline's daughter," she said, as Fearless jumped off her bike. "Are you any good?"

"I try my best," replied Fearless with a tight-lipped smile.

"I should hope so, too," said Beatrice Daisychain, setting off at a brisk waddle towards the cup cake houses. "Follow me!"

Fearless peered inside the first house. The room was round and decorated with rose-pink wallpaper and stripey silver curtains. In the middle was a four-poster bed with hangings the same as the curtains. Fearless gasped.

Lying on the bed was a large white poodle. It was chewing on a piece of sirloin steak and watching a film on the television. The film showed a collie dog sitting on a tree trunk, eyes shining, tail wagging. People were patting the dog and saying things like "Lassie, we love you," and "Lassie, you're wonderful."

Fearless stared with her mouth open. What on earth was going on?

She followed Beatrice Daisychain round each little house. It was the same room and the same film in each one.

"Why do your poodles watch *Lassie* films?" whispered Fearless.

Beatrice Daisychain fixed her with watery brown eyes. "ONLY WINNERS WIN!" she shouted. "If you FEEL good, you LOOK good."

"I beg your pardon?" said Fearless.

"Don't you know anything?" yelled Beatrice Daisychain. "Lassie is a WINNER and looks GOOD. My dogs are learning HOW!"

"I see," muttered Fearless, who had decided that not only was Beatrice Daisychain the rudest person she had ever met, but that Beatrice Daisychain was also completely mad.

At that moment a scrawny man, holding a gold lead, shambled across the grass. A dirty white overall came down to his knees and a grey parrot was perched on his shoulder. At the end of the lead was the strangest-looking dog Fearless had ever seen.

It was a beautifully-clipped, totally purple poodle wearing a magnificent jewelled collar. It was Lulu Labelle.

Poor Lulu Labelle! She didn't look very happy.

"Squib!" screamed Beatrice
Daisychain. "Randolph Squib! I've
been looking for you everywhere!"

The man in the overall looked
up. Randolph Squib took care of
Beatrice Daisychain's poodles. But
only because he adored poodles and
usually managed to avoid Beatrice
Daisychain.

"Yes?" he muttered.

"I know who did it," shouted Beatrice Daisychain.

"What?" cried Fearless. "Why didn't you tell me in the first place?"

"Because you never asked, you idiot!" shouted Beatrice Daisychain.

Fearless took a deep breath and counted to ten. It wouldn't do for a reporter on the *Daily Screamer* to lose her temper.

"Who was it?" she asked slowly.

"It was my horrible sister, Edwina Buzzard," screamed Beatrice Daisychain. "She wants to win the Top Dog Trophy instead of me."

"But that's impossible," said Fearless, who happened to have read the dog story in last week's *Daily Screamer*. "Edwina Buzzard breeds prize-winning bloodhounds. If she sabotaged your dog, she would be banned from entering the competition ever again."

"You ask her for yourself," snarled Beatrice Daisychain. "Then you'll know I'm telling the truth. Won't she, Squib?"

Randolph Squib acted as though he hadn't heard a single word. "I'm taking Lulu to see a film in the town," he said. "It is called *'They Came, They Conquered and They Were Purple'*." He paused. "I hope it will make her feel better."

"And me, Squib?" shouted Beatrice Daisychain. "What's going to make me feel better?"

Randolph Squib gave her a long, curious look. "How about a short swim in a swamp?" he suggested in a low voice.

Fearless Fiona looked from one to the other. Something was going on here and she had no idea what it was.

She ran to her bike. There was no point in asking Beatrice Daisychain any more questions. She had to talk to Edwina Buzzard.

Chapter Three

"Everyone's blaming me!" wailed
Edwina Buzzard. "But I didn't do it!"

She pulled a large purple handkerchief
from her shiny purple handbag and
blew her nose. "You must believe me
or it will be too late and Sir Jasper
Leatherjacket will ban me from
Krumbs forever!"

Fearless Fiona looked around her. Not only was the house painted purple on the outside, with purple roses climbing up the walls and purple net curtains at the windows, but everything was purple inside too. Including Edwina Buzzard. She had lilac hair and wore long purple earrings. A thick smear of frosted purple lipstick just missed her mouth.

Fearless thought of the colour of Lulu Labelle. Things didn't look too good for Edwina Buzzard. Fearless sat down on a purple satin sofa and pulled out her notebook.

"First things first," she said, firmly. "Who is Sir Jasper Leatherjacket?"

"He's the judge of the Top Dog Trophy at Krumbs and he's Lady Mothproof's brother," sniffed Edwina Buzzard.

"Why would everyone want to blame you?" asked Fearless.

"They're jealous," said Edwina Buzzard. She took out a purple whistle and blew it twice.

Suddenly the room was full of bloodhounds; big ones and medium-sized ones and one little one.

Not everybody likes bloodhounds. They have long, baggy faces and droopy, brown eyes. But there's nothing droopy about their noses. Some people call them newspaper hounds. One whiff of a story and

they're on the trail, snuffling like steam
trains and pulling at their leads.

"The problem is I always win the Top Dog Trophy," said Edwina Buzzard. "Someone decided to pour ink over poor Lulu Labelle and blame it on me so that I would be banned from the competition."

Edwina Buzzard turned to Fearless Fiona with wide open eyes. "I've been FRAMED!" she howled.

All the bloodhounds howled too.

Fearless stared at Edwina Buzzard. She really was a most peculiar purple sight, but even so, something came across loud and clear and Fearless recognised it immediately. Edwina Buzzard was telling the truth.

"I believe you," she said firmly. "But what you need is an alibi."

Edwina Buzzard looked confused. "Will it go with purple?" she asked.

Fearless tried again. "Where were you last night?" she asked.

"I was here," said Edwina Buzzard. "Watching the news with my bloodhounds."

"What?"

"A good reporter can smell out any story, no matter how well it's hidden," explained Edwina Buzzard. "My bloodhounds are learning to do the same."

"Of course," muttered Fearless who was beginning to think that Edwina Buzzard was just as mad as her sister.

"I know what to do!" cried Edwina Buzzard. "I'll write Sir Jasper a note explaining everything!" She picked up a pen and began to scribble furiously. "And you can take it to Mothproof Hall." Half an hour later, Fearless

Fiona pushed past the revolving doors of Mothproof Hall. She recognized Lady Mothproof immediately. She had a pineapple on her head and was wearing a long dress that looked as if it was made out of grass.

"You're better than any silly doggy-woggy, aren't you darling," cooed Lady Mothproof.

Fearless opened her mouth to speak then shut it quickly.

Lady Mothproof was talking to an enormous watermelon propped up against a pillow in an old-fashioned pram. "We'll speak to Sir Jasper," she murmured. "We'll say,

who gives a stuff about Top Dogs?
What about Top Watermelons, eh?"

"Excuse me," said Fearless Fiona.
"Would it be possible to speak to Sir
Jasper Leatherjacket?"

"Aren't you Fiona Jane Metalpress?"
cried Lady Mothproof.

Fearless Fiona nodded. "I have
an important letter for Sir Jasper
Leatherjacket," she said. "He must read
it immediately."

"He must and he will!" cried Lady Mothproof. "Come with me!"

Lady Mothproof propelled Fearless down a long corridor to the conservatory.

"Jasper!" she bellowed.

A bald-headed man turned towards them. He was huge and fat and his skin was a greenish grey colour.

"Looks just like a caterpillar, doesn't he?" cried Lady Mothproof. "Always has done. Ever since

he was a baby!" She threw back her head and roared with laughter. "All Leatherjackets do, you know!"

Fearless looked around the room. Lord Mothproof was holding a moth-eaten whippet. The Mayoress had a chihuahua on the end of a red silk dressing gown cord. Mr Stinge, the bank manager, was whispering into the black, floppy ear of an enormous basset hound. Even Crinoline and Lacy, the Mothproofs' daughters, were prancing about with two silly-looking dalmatians.

All these people want to win the Top Dog Trophy, thought Fearless in amazement. Any one of them could have dyed Lulu Labelle purple!

"Well?" drawled Sir Jasper Leatherjacket, moving towards her. "What is it now?"

Fearless handed him the note. "I've spoken to Edwina Buzzard," she said breathlessly. "I'm sure she's innocent."

Sir Jasper looked at her over his round spectacles. His eyebrows were long and hairy and they stuck out like feelers in front of his head.

"Are you?" he said in a snooty voice.

Fearless Fiona decided she didn't like Sir Jasper Leatherjacket one little bit.

"Yes, I am," she said.

She watched as he ripped open the envelope and held the note under a lamp.

"Look here," he said. "This purple ink is exactly the same colour as the ink that was poured over that poor poodle!" He thrust the note back at

Fearless. "Of course it was her!"

Fearless stared at the writing on the page. Sir Jasper Leatherjacket was right! It was the same colour!

"There must be some mistake," she said, quickly. "Edwina Buzzard . . ."

Sir Jasper held up a fat doughy finger. "Edwina Buzzard is banned from Krumbs," he said. "And that is that."

Fearless ran from the room. Her head was spinning. She was still sure that Edwina Buzzard was innocent, but how could she prove it in time?

Chapter Four

"Fiona Jane!" cried Mrs Metalpress. "I need your help!"

She was standing in the kitchen, holding Tinytoes, her Yorkshire terrier. Laid out on the table were twelve little jackets. There were gold ones with silver buttons and silver ones with gold buttons. There were stripy blue ones and spotty yellow ones. To go with each jacket, there were twelve little matching bows.

Fearless stared at them. She wondered if her mother had somehow got stuck on her sewing machine like a needle gets stuck on a record and plays the same thing again and again.

"What's your problem, Mum?" she asked.

"Which one shall I choose?" said Mrs Metalpress breathlessly. "Tinytoes needs to look her best for the Top Dog Trophy this evening."

"How about the green satin one embroidered with the silver dog biscuits," said a dark-haired boy in a long T-shirt and a baseball cap.

Fearless turned around.

"Whizzkid!" she yelled. "Am I glad to see you!"

Whizzkid Wayne was her favourite

cousin on her father's side. He was a computer wizard, a genius with his chemistry set, but most important of all, he was a handwriting expert.

"What's up?" said Whizzkid Wayne.

Fearless pulled Edwina Buzzard's letter out of her top pocket. "Read this," she said. "Is she telling the truth?"

Whizzkid lifted the magnifying glass he always wore around his neck. He moved it backwards and forwards over Edwina Buzzard's round, purple writing.

There were no wobbly lines and

no guilty-looking blobs. He handed it back to Fearless. "She's not lying," he said, firmly.

"Thank goodness," said Fearless. "Now all we have to do is find out who is."

"What are you talking about?" asked Whizzkid Wayne.

"Whaddya know about poodles?" said Fearless with a grin. And she told him the whole story.

"Fearless!" cried Mrs Metalpress. "There's a purple poodle sitting on the front doorstep!"

"Colliding computers!" cried Whizzkid Wayne when he saw Lulu Labelle. "What's she doing here?"

"I don't know," said Fearless. "But someone is trying to tell me something and I think I know who that someone is."

Whizzkid patted Lulu Labelle's head. Then he looked at the purple stain on his fingers.

"It's permanent ink," said Fearless. "No one can get it out."

Whizzkid Wayne looked at the stain through his magnifying glass.

Fearless held her breath.

"Whizzkid?" she said slowly. "Can you do it?"

There was a strange faraway look on Whizzkid's face.

"I think so," he said.

"What do you need?" asked Fearless.

"My chemistry set and your bathtub," said Whizzkid Wayne.

"You've got it!" cried Fearless. Then she pulled on her white catsuit and slung a coil of rope over her shoulder.

"Where are you going?" asked Whizzkid.

"To get some answers," said Fearless. "Meet me at the Competition."

Chapter Five

All the way to Poodles' Paradise, Fearless thought about Randolph Squib. There was something very peculiar about him and she had to find out what it was.

She flipped her bike into top gear. There was no time to lose.

As Fearless had expected, the gates to Poodles' Paradise were locked. She uncoiled her rope, tied a loop in one end and threw a perfect lasso into the air. It landed neatly around the head of an iron poodle. She pulled the rope tight and began to climb.

It was strangely quiet up at the big pink and white house. The poodles were still watching *Lassie* but there was

no sign of either Beatrice Daisychain
or Randolph Squib.

Fearless tiptoed round the back.
Ahead of her was an archway leading
into a small courtyard.

NO ENTRY ESPECIALLY YOU
BEATRICE DAISYCHAIN

was printed in big black letters over
the top. Across the courtyard was

a white door with *Randolph Squib* written on it in gold letters. Fearless pulled on the bell rope.

There was a loud jangling noise but nobody answered.

Fearless's heart sank. Without talking to Randolph Squib, she didn't have a hope of saving Edwina Buzzard. What's more there would be no dog story for tomorrow's *Daily Screamer*.

She began to walk slowly back across the courtyard.

"The key's in the flowerpot! The key's in the flowerpot!" screeched a voice.

Fearless nearly jumped out of her skin.

Randolph Squib's grey parrot swooped down in front her and landed on the edge of a big stone flower pot.

"The key's in the flowerpot! The key's in the flowerpot!"

Fearless bent down. Sure enough at the bottom of the flowerpot under a pile of leaves was a long metal key. She picked it up and went back to Randolph Squib's door. With a thumping heart, she put the key in the lock.

Now what shall I do, thought
Fearless Fiona. Going into other
people's houses without asking
them is no way to behave. Then
she remembered something Edwina
Buzzard had said about good reporters
smelling out stories. She took a deep
breath, turned the key in the lock and
opened the door.

Fearless Fiona gasped. Randolph
Squib's room was entirely purple!
It was exactly the same purple as
Edwina Buzzard's house. But the most
astonishing thing of all was hanging
on the wall opposite the front door.
Fearless crossed the room to get a
better look.

It was a huge purple satin heart with
a picture of Edwina Buzzard in the
middle.

She looked around the room. On every table, Edwina Buzzard's face looked out of heart-shaped frames!

Why would Randolph Squib still work for Beatrice Daisychain and keep pictures of Edwina Buzzard in his room? Especially heart-shaped ones. It didn't make any sense.

"He's too shy to tell her! He's too

shy to tell her!" screeched a voice. The parrot perched on the edge of the table and cocked a shiny yellow eye at her.

Then Fearless saw the note.

Dear Fearless Fiona,
Bring the parrot to the judges' tent.
It's Edwina Buzzard's last chance.
Your Faithful servant,
Randolph Squib

There was no time to wonder why. Fearless grabbed the parrot and stuffed it in a pillow case. Then she ran back down the drive, leapt over the gate and jumped on to her bike.

Whizzkid Wayne was standing at the back door of the Competition Hall. Beside him was a magnificent snowy-white poodle wearing a jewelled collar.

Fearless couldn't believe her eyes!

"How did you do it?" she cried.

"First I had to convince your mother that if she had a purple bathtub everyone else would want one," said Whizzkid Wayne with a grin. "After that it was easy."

"Ladies and gentlemen!" boomed a voice. "The competition has begun!"

"Quick," said Fearless. "Take off Lulu's collar! Then nobody will know who she is!"

Inside the Hall, people and dogs were walking round in a big circle.

Fearless could see Lord Mothproof, the Mayoress, Mr Stinge, the bank manager and Crinoline and Lacy. Even her mother was there clutching

Tinytoes. And in a corner looking pale and purple was Edwina Buzzard.

Fearless nodded at Whizzkid Wayne who quickly joined the procession with Lulu Labelle.

Halfway round the circle Sir Jasper Leatherjacket was talking to Lady Mothproof. The two of them were bent over an old-fashioned pram and Sir Jasper was looking inside and shaking his head. Lady Mothproof was pinching him and pulling his hair.

Beside them stood Randolph Squib in his dirty white overall, but neither of them paid any attention to him.

"Squib!" bellowed a voice. "Where is she?"

Beatrice Daisychain stumped across the tent.

Randolph Squib turned to face her.

"If you are referring to Lulu," he said in an icy voice, "she's in much safer hands than yours."

Edwina Buzzard's head jerked up. She ran into the middle of the circle.

"You did it," she shouted at her sister. "You've always been jealous of me!"

"No I didn't!" screamed Beatrice Daisychain.

"Yes you did!" yelled Edwina Buzzard.

"Didn't."

"Did."

"Didn't."

"Did."

The two sisters glared at each other.

"Prove it,"

snarled Beatrice Daisychain. There was a triumphant sneer on her puggy face.

Fearless Fiona caught Randolph Squib's eye. She opened the pillow case and the parrot fluttered into the air. It swooped down and landed on Beatrice Daisychain's head.

"Take off your gloves! Take off your gloves!" it screeched.

The entire tent went quiet. Even the dogs stopped whining.

Edwina Buzzard grabbed Beatrice Daisychain by the left arm. Randolph

Squib grabbed the right one. With
two sharp tugs they pulled
off her long white gloves.
Fearless gasped. Beatrice
Daisychain's hands and
forearms were stained
with purple ink – the
same purple ink that
had been poured over
Lulu Labelle.

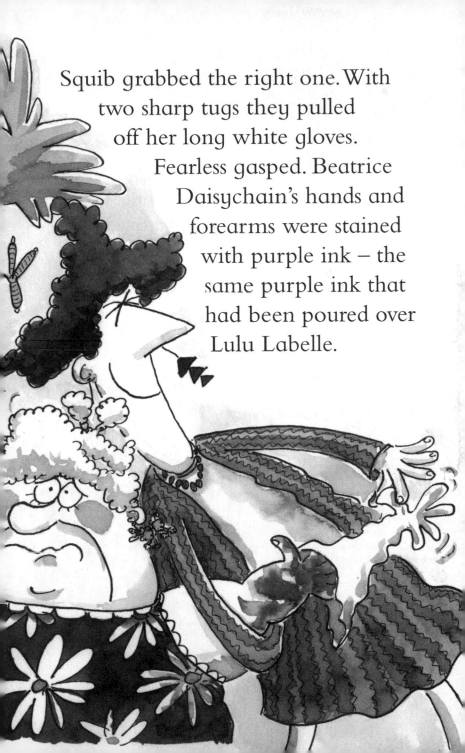

At that very moment, Sir Jasper Leatherjacket walked up to the microphone.

"The winner of the Top Dog Trophy is Whizzkid Wayne," he boomed.

Beatrice Daisychain took one look at the winning poodle, let out a strangled cry and collapsed in a heap on the ground.

Sir Jasper Leatherjacket looked from Beatrice Daisychain to Edwina Buzzard and back again. Then he went red in the face and began to rattle like a boiler about to explode.

"Will someone tell me what is going on?"

he bellowed.

Randolph Squib and Edwina Buzzard said nothing. They were holding hands and staring at their feet.

"I will," said Fearless Fiona in a loud voice. And she walked up to Sir Jasper Leatherjacket, looked him straight in the eye and told him the whole story.

Sir Jasper Leatherjacket was stunned.

"I'm sorry," he mumbled to Fearless Fiona. "I owe you an apology."

"And I owe you more than that."

Fearless turned around. Edwina Buzzard was holding a bloodhound puppy in her arms. "He's called Lucky," she said with her

frosted-purple smile. "I want you to have him."

Fearless was speechless. She had wanted one of Edwina Buzzard's bloodhounds from the first moment she had seen them. "Thank you," she stammered. "I . . ."

Outside the tent a telephone began to ring.

Fearless Fiona knew which one it was. She ran to her bike and grabbed the mobile phone from its clip.

"Didya get the dog story?" growled Deadline Metalpress.

"Sure did," said Fearless Fiona. "I got the story! And I got the dog!"

"You're the greatest," growled Deadline Metalpress.

As he spoke the bloodhound puppy snuffled round the corner of the tent and clambered on to Fearless Fiona's knee.

"It was easy," she said with a big grin. "I got Lucky!"